I Like
Old Clothes

by **Mary Ann Hoberman**

illustrations by **Patrice Barton**

Alfred A. Knopf

New York

THIS IS A BORZOI BOOK PUBLISHED BY ALFRED A. KNOPF

Visit us on the Web! randomhouse.com/kids

Educators and librarians, for a variety of teaching tools, visit us at
randomhouse.com/teachers

Library of Congress Cataloging-in-Publication Data
Hoberman, Mary Ann.
I like old clothes / by Mary Ann Hoberman ; illustrations by Patrice Barton.
p.   cm.
"Originally published with different illustrations by Alfred A. Knopf in 1976"—Copyright p.
Summary: A child who likes wearing hand-me-downs imagines in verse the history of these clothes.
ISBN 978-0-375-86951-8 (trade) — ISBN 978-0-375-96951-5 (lib. bdg.)
[1. Stories in rhyme. 2. Clothing and dress—Fiction.] I. Barton, Patrice, ill. II. Title.
PZ8.3.H66Iab 2012
[E]—dc22
2010038292

The text of this book is set in 18-point Mrs. Eaves.
The illustrations were created using pencil sketches and mixed media, assembled and painted digitally.

MANUFACTURED IN MALAYSIA
August 2012
10 9 8 7 6 5 4 3 2 1

First Edition

For my granddaughters Dorothy and Kit
(who really like old clothes)
—M.A.H.

For my son, Seth, with love
—P.B.

I like old clothes,
Hand-me-down clothes,
Worn outgrown clothes,
Not-my-own clothes.

When somebody grows
And gives me her clothes,
I don't say, "What, *those*?"
And turn up my nose
The way some people do
When their clothes aren't new.

I *like* old clothes.
I really do.

Clothes with a history,
Clothes with a mystery,

Sweaters and shirts

That are brother-and-sistery,

Clothes that belonged to a friend of a friend,

Who wore them to school when she lived in East Bend.

"You lived in East Bend once, Blue Sweater," I say.

"Just think, you are living in my town today."

I like old clothes,
Everyday clothes,
Once-for-good clothes,
Now-for-play clothes.

When I wear them,

Then I say, "Clothes,

I wonder who wore you before you were mine?

Was she light-haired or dark-haired, seven or nine?

Did you make her look awful or make her look fine?"

It's hard to tell
Who'd look well
In a yellow dress,
Who would look a mess
In a red-striped hat.
"Was she thin or fat?
Did she have a cat?"
I ask them that.

I like old clothes,

Cozy warm clothes,

Broken-in clothes,

Where've-you-been clothes,

Clothes that were worn

Before I was born

And now are mine.

Skirts with the line
Of a let-down hem,
I like *them*!
And party dresses
Not quite new,
Not quite in style,
I like them, too.

I like to wonder what they've done,

What games they've played

And if they won,

And if the parties turned out fun.

I like old clothes,
Faded-out clothes,
Not-so-new clothes,
Where-were-you clothes.

And each time I wear them
I try to imagine
The places they've been
And the faces they've seen—

And whose clothes they'll be

When they've finished with me.